WELCOME TO
PASSPORT TO READING
A beginning reader's ticket to a brand-new world!

Every book in this program is designed to build read-along and read-alone skills, level by level, through engaging and enriching stories. As the reader turns each page, he or she will become more confident with new vocabulary, sight words, and comprehension.

These PASSPORT TO READING levels will help you choose the perfect book for every reader.

READING TOGETHER
Read short words in simple sentence structures together to begin a reader's journey.

READING OUT LOUD
Encourage developing readers to sound out words in more complex stories with simple vocabulary.

READING INDEPENDENTLY
Newly independent readers gain confidence reading more complex sentences with higher word counts.

READY TO READ MORE
Readers prepare for chapter books with fewer illustrations and longer paragraphs.

This book features sight words from the educator-supported Dolch Sight Words List. This encourages the reader to recognize commonly used vocabulary words, increasing reading speed and fluency.

For more information, please visit passporttoreadingbooks.com.

Enjoy the journey!

PONYVILLE
READING ADVENTURES

LITTLE, BROWN AND COMPANY
New York Boston

Little, Brown and Company

Hachette Book Group
1290 Avenue of the Americas, New York, NY 10104
Visit us at lb-kids.com

Little, Brown and Company is a division of Hachette Book Group, Inc.
The Little, Brown name and logo are trademarks of
Hachette Book Group, Inc.

The publisher is not responsible for websites (or their content)
that are not owned by the publisher.

First Edition: July 2015

Meet the Ponies of Ponyville, Hearts and Hooves, and *Holly, Jolly Harmony*
originally published in 2013 by Little, Brown and Company.
Ponies Love Pets! and *Meet the Princess of Friendship* originally
published in 2014 by Little, Brown and Company.
Power Ponies to the Rescue! originally published
in 2015 by Little, Brown and Company.

ISBN 978-0-316-33740-3 (paper over board) — ISBN 978-0-316-41084-7 (pb)

10 9 8 7 6 5 4 3 2 1

SC

Printed in China

Passport to Reading titles are leveled by independent reviewers applying the standards developed by Irene Fountas and Gay Su Pinnell in *Matching Books to Readers: Using Leveled Books in Guided Reading,* Heinemann, 1999.

Table of Contents

MEET THE PONIES OF PONYVILLE

by Olivia London

LITTLE, BROWN AND COMPANY
New York   Boston

Attention, My Little Pony fans!
Look for these items when you read this story.
Can you spot them all?

unicorn

letter

orchard

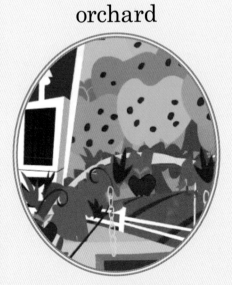

dragon

In the center of Equestria
is the busy town of Ponyville.
Ponyville is a place
where all kinds of ponies
live together in peace.

Everypony who comes to visit leaves with many new friends! Let us meet the ponies of Ponyville and learn why everypony loves them!

Twilight Sparkle is a Unicorn.
She has strong magical powers,
stronger than most Unicorns.

Twilight loves to learn new things.
Princess Celestia is her teacher.
She sent Twilight to Ponyville
to study friendship.

Each week, Twilight has homework.
She writes letters to the princess
about her lessons on friendship.
Twilight always makes sure
her homework is in on time!

Twilight has already learned
that everypony needs friends.
Now she has five best friends!

Spike is a baby dragon.
He lives in the library
with Twilight Sparkle.

He helps Twilight with everything!
Spike even helps her
find books to read for fun!

Spike also helps
Twilight with her homework.
He has a magical way of sending
Twilight's letters to the princess.

Spike loves eating stones that sparkle!
Oh, and he has a secret crush on Rarity.
Shhh!

Rarity is a Unicorn.

She is a fashion designer.

She makes a dress for Twilight Sparkle.

Rarity uses her power to find
rare stones for the dress.
She says,
"I do not like it—I love it!"

Rarity owns the Carousel Boutique.

That is where she sells her clothes.

She collects pretty things.

Her cat, Opal, does, too!

Rarity likes to give gifts.

She made everypony the perfect dress
for the Grand Galloping Gala.

Applejack's dress looks fancy!

Applejack loves apples!
She works in the orchard
at Sweet Apple Acres.
Her dog, Winona, helps on the farm!

The Apple family makes a lot
of yummy food at the farm.
Applejack often sells the food
at the Ponyville market.

Applejack works hard.

She always tells the truth.

Applejack cheers at the rodeo!

She likes to yell "Yee-haw!"

Applejack loves playing games,
but she prefers to win—
just like Rainbow Dash!

Rainbow Dash flies fast—
faster than anyone else!
She hopes to be on the
Wonderbolts flying team!

Rainbow Dash can fly so fast
that she can change the weather.

Rainbow Dash is a good friend.
But she also likes playing tricks
on other ponies!

She was born in Cloudsdale,
just like Fluttershy!

Fluttershy is graceful and kind.
She adores all animals.
Fluttershy lives near the forest
with her bunny, Angel.

Fluttershy has a special skill
called the Stare.
It calms down wild animals—
even full-grown dragons!

She is shy around other ponies.
It is hard to hear Fluttershy
when she speaks.
She is not like Pinkie Pie!

Pinkie Pie has a lot of energy!
She loves to giggle and sing.
She bakes treats for the
Sugarcube Corner bakery.

Pinkie Pie makes ponies smile.
She always says,
"You know what this calls for?
A party!"

Now you know what makes
the Ponyville ponies special.
Come back and visit them soon!

HEARTS AND HOOVES

Adapted by Jennifer Fox

Based on the episode "Hearts and Hooves Day"

written by Meghan McCarthy

LITTLE, BROWN AND COMPANY

New York   Boston

Attention, My Little Pony fans!
Look for these items when you read this story.
Can you spot them all?

valentine

smelly

picnic

potion

The Cutie Mark Crusaders
are making a valentine for their
favorite teacher, Miss Cheerilee.

"More lace!" says Sweetie Belle.

"More hoof prints!" says Apple Bloom.

"More glitter!" says Scootaloo.

Hearts and Hooves Day
only comes once a year.

They want Miss Cheerilee to have

the best one ever!

The ponies give their teacher the valentine.

"Do you have a very
special somepony?"
Sweetie Belle asks Miss Cheerilee.

"No," Miss Cheerilee says.

The Cutie Mark Crusaders get an idea!

"We will find her a special
somepony," they say.

They do not have much time.
Hearts and Hooves Day
is almost over.

They have to find the perfect
stallion for Miss Cheerilee.
Not too silly.
Not too flashy.
Not too smelly.

43

"He is the one!" says Scootaloo.

She nods at Big McIntosh.

"My brother?" asks Apple Bloom.

"Big Mac is nice,
and he works hard,"
says Scootaloo.
"They will fall in love,"
says Apple Bloom.

The Cutie Mark Crusaders
set up a picnic date for
Big Mac and Miss Cheerilee.
But they do not fall in love.

Later, the ponies see
Twilight Sparkle.
She has a book
about love potions.
It gives them a new idea!

They mix up a love potion
for Big Mac and Miss Cheerilee.

Miss Cheerilee and Big Mac
drink the love potion.

Big Mac and Miss Cheerilee
fall in love right away.
They call each other
silly names like Pony Pie
and Shmoopie Moopie.

"It worked!" the ponies cheer.

But Big Mac and Miss Cheerilee
are TOO much in love.
They stare at each other all day.
They are not themselves.
They even decide to get married!

"We made a mistake,"
says Apple Bloom.
"We need to undo the spell
that the potion put on them."

To break the spell, the ponies
have to keep Big Mac and
Miss Cheerilee apart for one hour.
"We should go plan your wedding!"
they tell Miss Cheerilee.

Time passes, and the spell is broken!
Miss Cheerilee and Big Mac
are back to normal.
"I hope you have learned something.
Everypony has to find their own special
somepony," says Miss Cheerilee.

HOLLY, JOLLY HARMONY

Adapted by D. Jakobs

Based on the episode "Hearth's Warming Eve"
written by Merriwether Williams

LITTLE, BROWN AND COMPANY
New York   Boston

Attention, My Little Pony fans!
Look for these items when you read this story.
Can you spot them all?

wreath

tree

food

Windigo

The pony friends love the holiday
called Hearth's Warming Eve.
It is a time of harmony and friendship.

The ponies of Canterlot
decorate each wreath and tree
with stars, bells, and ribbons.
The city looks so pretty!

Each year,

the ponies and Spike put on a show.

The ponies play different parts

while Spike tells the story.

Once, there were three pony tribes.

The leaders of the Earth Ponies, the Pegasi,

and the Unicorns were named

Chancellor Puddinghead,

Commander Hurricane, and Princess Platinum.

The Pegasi made the weather.

The Earth Ponies grew the food.

The Unicorns used magic
to make day and night.

This was not a happy time.

The three tribes did not get along.

Then one day a huge snowstorm

stopped the crops from growing.

Everypony was running out of food!

The three tribe leaders blamed one another.

The meaner they were,

the harder it snowed.

Each leader decided to find a new land for her tribe.

Private Pansy went with
Commander Hurricane.
Flying in the snowstorm
was scary.

Princess Platinum was glad
to leave the others.
"Do you agree?"
she asked Clover the Clever.
"We could have tried harder,"
Clover answered.

Smart Cookie and Chancellor Puddinghead
kept getting lost.
Puddinghead might have been using
her map wrong.

All the ponies found new homes
for their tribes.

"I name this land Pegasopolis,"
said Hurricane.

"I am double-dazzled
by all these jewels,"
said Princess Platinum.
"I name this land Unicornia!"

"This dirt is the dirtiest!
I name this land Dirtville!"
said a happy Puddinghead.
"How about we call it Earth?"
asked Smart Cookie.

But each tribe leader had
chosen the same land!
"I planted my flag first!"
"Did not!"
"Did too!" they argued.

As the pony leaders yelled,
snow and winds appeared.
"Oh no!" said Hurricane.
"Not again!"

Instead of beautiful,
it was blizzardy.
Instead of wonderful,
it was wintry.
Instead of spectacular,
it was snow-tacular.

The ponies needed a safe place
to hide from the storm.
The only shelter was a cave.

"Earth Ponies are fools!"
said Hurricane.

"Unicorns are snobs!"
said Puddinghead.

"Pegasi are brutes!"
said Platinum.

When the pony leaders called
one another mean names,
they were frozen in ice.

The other ponies heard wails
coming from outside the cave.
"It is a Windigo!" said Clover.
"A Windigo is a winter spirit
who feeds on hate.
It froze our leaders!"

"I do not hate you," said Pansy.

"Me neither," Clover agreed.

"It does not matter if we are different. We are all ponies!" said Cookie.

A pinkish-purple heart burst
from Clover's horn.

It chased away the Windigo.

The ice began to melt.

"This magic came from
all three of us," said Clover.
"We joined together in friendship!"

All three tribes became friends.
They sang songs that became
the winter carols everypony
still sings today.

Ponies have been kind
to one another ever since.
Together, they named
their new land Equestria!
And that is the story
of Hearth's Warming Eve.

PONIES LOVE PETS!

by Emily C. Hughes

LITTLE, BROWN AND COMPANY
New York   Boston

Attention, My Little Pony fans!
Look for these items when you read this story.
Can you spot them all?

alligator

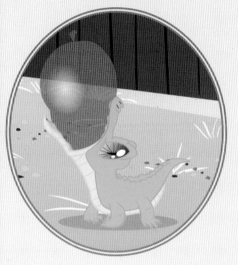

cattle

tortoise

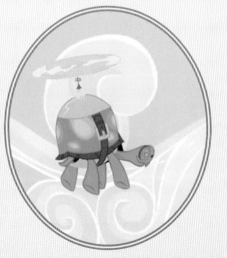

phoenix

These ponies are best friends.

They love to laugh together.

They also love to play with their pets!

The ponies and their pets are
always there to help one another.

Angel is Fluttershy's pet bunny.

He can be a little bossy.

But Angel makes Fluttershy
feel better when she is sad.

Pinkie Pie has a pet alligator named Gummy.
Most ponies would not want an alligator
for a pet, but Gummy is special.
He has no teeth!

It is lucky because he LOVES to bite!

Twilight Sparkle has Owlowiscious.
He helps her by bringing books from
the library.

At first, he and Spike did not get along,
but now they are good friends.

A pony like Applejack needs
a good work dog like Winona!
Winona helps the Apple family
herd the cattle.

The Apple family got Winona
when she was a puppy.
She loves to run and leap and
have her belly scratched!

Rainbow Dash wants a pet as fast and cool as she is, like a falcon or a bat.

She has a contest to find the best animal.
Fluttershy has lots of ideas.

Soon Rainbow Dash meets Tank,
a tortoise who saves her
when a rock falls on her wing.

Tank may be slow,

but Rainbow Dash fixes that.

She turns him into a flying tortoise!

Opalescence is Rarity's cat.
She helps make beautiful
dresses for the other ponies.

The cat does not like to get wet.

She also does not like to do chores.

But there is nothing she hates
more than when someone tries
to steal her toys!

It is not just the ponies of Ponyville
who have pets.

Princess Celestia has a phoenix
named Philomena.

Philomena has a special talent.

She can burst into flames!

Philomena sometimes uses that talent to play tricks on the ponies. Fluttershy has never seen anything like it!

Even Spike has a pet.

Peewee is a baby phoenix.

Spike rescued Peewee back
when he was still an egg.

Pets are hard work!

But the ponies love them.

And the pets love the ponies!

Because friendship is magic, and
pets are a very special kind of friend!

MEET THE

PRINCESS OF FRIENDSHIP

Adapted by Lucy Rosen

Based on the episodes

"Twilight's Kingdom – Parts 1 and 2"

written by Meghan McCarthy

LITTLE, BROWN AND COMPANY

New York   Boston

Attention, My Little Pony fans!
Look for these items when you read
this story. Can you spot them all?

princess

moon

castle

throne

Princess Twilight Sparkle is the
newest princess in Equestria.

Twilight Sparkle was
not always a princess.
She came to Ponyville
to learn about friendship
and to study magic.

One day, Twilight Sparkle
used magic to help her friends.
She cast a brand-new spell
and saved the day.

Nopony had ever created new magic
with the power of friendship before!

Princess Celestia was so proud.
She had always known
that Twilight Sparkle
was a very special pony.

"Now you are ready to fulfill
your destiny," Princess Celestia
told Twilight Sparkle.

A beam of light swirled
around Twilight Sparkle.
When it cleared,
Twilight Sparkle looked different.
She was an Alicorn,
a Unicorn with wings!

"You look like a princess,"
Fluttershy whispered.
"Now she is one,"
said Princess Celestia.

That is how Princess Twilight
became one of the four leaders
of Equestria.

Together, these leaders
make sure the ponies
live together in peace
and harmony.

Princess Celestia lives in Canterlot
with her sister, Princess Luna.
They used to fight,
but now they are as close as can be.

134

They make the sun and moon
rise and set each day.

Princess Cadance
rules the Crystal Empire.
She is married to Shining Armor.
He is Princess Twilight's brother!

Princess Twilight is proud to lead
with the other royal ponies.
But she is not sure what
it means to be a princess.

Princess Twilight does not have
a special job like the others.
She does not have a castle
like the others.
All she does is smile and wave.

One day, an evil creature
comes to Equestria.
It is Tirek.
He is out to steal
everypony's magic!

Nopony can stop him,

not even the other princesses.

But Princess Twilight has a plan.

She knows there is something
even stronger than Tirek.
It is the power of friendship!

Princess Twilight gathers her friends.
Rainbow Dash, Pinkie Pie,
Rarity, Applejack, and
Fluttershy give all their
might to defeat the evil villain.

With the help of her friends,
Princess Twilight releases
rainbow power.

A flash of light
blinds the ponies.
When they open their eyes,
they cannot believe what they see!

Where Tirek once stood,
there is now a beautiful castle.
"It belongs to you, Princess Twilight,"
says Princess Celestia.

The friends are in awe.

Inside the castle,

there are six thrones,

one for each pony.

There is even a throne for Spike!

"Now do you understand
what you are meant to do
as a princess?"
asks Princess Celestia.

Princess Twilight smiles.

"Yes," she says.

"I am meant to spread
the magic of friendship
all across Equestria."

"That makes you
the princess of friendship,"
says Princess Celestia.

At last, Princess Twilight
knows her destiny.
And what is the princess of friendship
without her friends by her side?

POWER PONIES
TO THE RESCUE!

Adapted by Magnolia Belle
Based on the episode "Power Ponies"
written by Meghan McCarthy,
Charlotte Fullerton & Betsy McGowen

LITTLE, BROWN AND COMPANY
New York   Boston

Attention, My Little Pony fans! Look for these words when you read this story. Can you spot them all?

comic

costumes

mailbox

lightning

Everypony is hard at work.
The friends are cleaning
Luna and Celestia's castle.

"Is there anything I can help
you with?" Spike asks.
"No, thank you!" Twilight says.

Spike finds a quiet place
to read his comic book.

Soon, the ponies look for Spike.

They want to share some snacks.

They find him reading a
secret message out loud.
"Take a closer look to join the
adventure in this book," Spike says.

The words are magic
and pull the ponies and
Spike into the book!

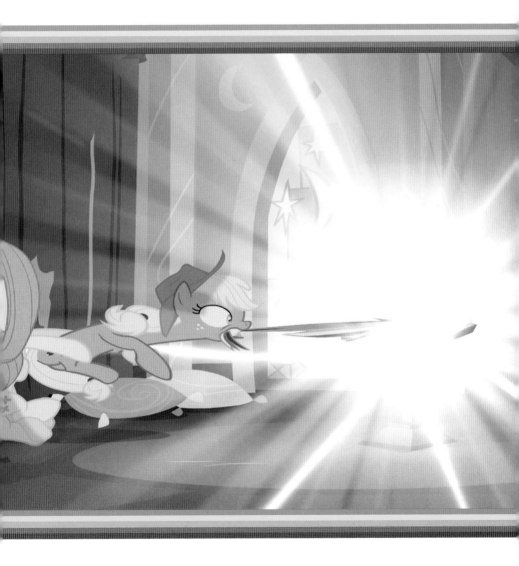

They are not in Ponyville anymore.
They are in a city called Maretropolis
and are all wearing costumes.
It is like they are inside Spike's
comic book.

"You are the superheroes
from my comic book!
It zapped us here somehow!"
says Spike.

"Power Ponies! You think you can stop me?" asks the crazy villain known as the Mane-iac.

"Did she just call us Power Ponies?" asks Applejack.

Spike knows the evil purple pony.
She is from his comic book.

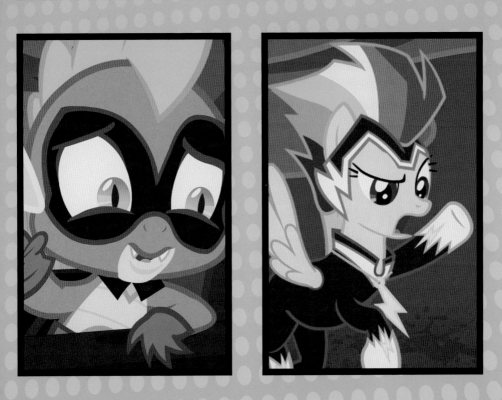

"Somepony zap us back!"
shouts Rainbow Dash.
"The comic says the only way out is
to defeat the Mane-iac!" says Spike.

The Mane-iac wants to fight.
She uses her hair to throw things
at the Power Ponies.
Pinkie Pie runs from a mailbox.

The Power Ponies use their skills
against the Mane-iac.
Applejack tries to catch her
with a golden lasso.
Twilight tries to shoot a freeze ray
from her horn.

Rainbow Dash tries to
make lightning.
Instead, she makes a tornado
that swallows all the ponies!
The Mane-iac escapes
with a glowing ball.

"Oh no!
The Mane-iac
got away with
the Electro Orb.
She can use
that to destroy
Maretropolis,"
says Spike.

"No biggie.
We are awesome.
We have superpowers!"
says Rainbow Dash.

"I do not have any," says Spike.

Twilight reminds Spike he is the only one who knows Maretropolis. He leads the team to the Mane-iac's secret base. "Is that a shampoo factory?" Pinkie Pie asks.

"Come on out, Mane-iac, or the Power Ponies are coming in!" shouts Applejack.

The Power Ponies battle
the Mane-iac's henchponies.
The heroes are about to win.
Then the Mane-iac uses a secret weapon!

HAIR SPRAY OF DOOM

She stops all the ponies,
but she does not stop Spike.
"It would be pointless to spray
you," the Mane-iac says.

Spike sneaks into the Mane-iac's base through a vent.

"How am I supposed to help my friends?" he asks himself.

"This cannon will cause the mane of everypony in Maretropolis to grow wild," says the Mane-iac.

"Are you forgetting about somepony?" asks Fluttershy.

The Mane-iac laughs and says,

"Little guy?

No superpowers?"

"He always comes through for us," says Twilight.

Twilight's words make Spike brave.
He distracts the Mane-iac's henchponies
and sets the Power Ponies free!

The Power Ponies then work together
to capture the crooks.
They can leave Maretropolis!

The friends celebrate in Ponyville.
"You do not have to have superpowers
to be a super friend," says Spike.
The friends all cheer and eat cupcakes.

DON'T MISS THESE OTHER PONYRIFFIC BOOKS!

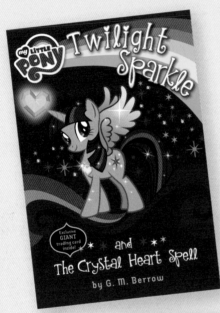

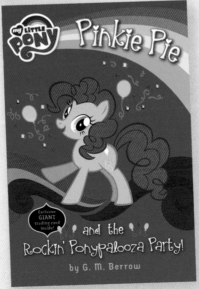

CHECK OUT THESE PONYRIFFIC BOOKS, TOO!

CHECKPOINTS IN THIS BOOK ✔

MEET THE PONIES OF PONYVILLE

WORD COUNT	GUIDED READING LEVEL	NUMBER OF DOLCH SIGHT WORDS
491	L	77

HEARTS AND HOOVES

WORD COUNT	GUIDED READING LEVEL	NUMBER OF DOLCH SIGHT WORDS
350	K	65

HOLLY, JOLLY HARMONY

WORD COUNT	GUIDED READING LEVEL	NUMBER OF DOLCH SIGHT WORDS
493	L	85

PONIES LOVE PETS!

WORD COUNT	GUIDED READING LEVEL	NUMBER OF DOLCH SIGHT WORDS
375	L	74

MEET THE PRINCESS OF FRIENDSHIP

WORD COUNT	GUIDED READING LEVEL	NUMBER OF DOLCH SIGHT WORDS
459	J	73

POWER PONIES TO THE RESCUE!

WORD COUNT	GUIDED READING LEVEL	NUMBER OF DOLCH SIGHT WORDS
533	K	89